Spaghetti for Suzy

Peta Coplans

MAMMOTH

For Cleo and Adam

This MAMMOTH belongs to

_____

_____

_____

Suzy liked lots of things – dogs, cats, balloons, fun-fairs and crazy bows in her hair.

At the park Suzy liked to build the highest castle in
the sand-pit . . .

. . . and then squash it flat.

Most of all, Suzy liked spaghetti. She ate it every day.
"One day she'll get tired of it," her mum said.

But she didn't. Soon she wouldn't eat anything else.

Every morning Suzy's mum cooked her a mountain of spaghetti.

By bedtime it was gone.
"She'll turn into a noodle soon," her dad said. But she didn't.

In the park one day, Suzy met a cat.
"Spaghetti! Just what I need!" said the cat.

He took a long piece . . .

What do you think he did with it?

Later, Suzy met a pig.
"Spaghetti! Just what I need!" said the pig, taking two
pieces . . .

What do you think he did with them?

Along came a dog.
"Spaghetti! Just what I need!" said the dog.

He emptied the whole bowlful into his bag . . .

What do you think he did with it?

"Thanks for the spaghetti," said Suzy's friends when they came back.

"We thought you might be hungry."

Suzy looked at the fruit. The animals looked at Suzy.

"Why fruit?" asked Suzy. "I only like spaghetti."

"Apples taste of windy autumn days," said the pig.

"Cherries taste of country picnics," said the cat.

"And bananas," said the dog, "bananas taste of the wild, green jungle."

"Hmm!" said Suzy, and she ate the fruit. "ALMOST as good as spaghetti!"

"I'm still hungry," said Suzy. "We're ALL hungry!"
said the dog.

"Well, come on," said Suzy. "What are we waiting for?"

"Spaghetti for everyone!" said Suzy.

And what do you think they did with it?

First published in Great Britain 1992
by Anderson Press Ltd
Published 1994 by Mammoth
an imprint of Reed Consumer Books Ltd
Michelin House, 81 Fulham Road, London SW3 6RB
and Auckland, Melbourne, Singapore and Toronto

ISBN 0 7497 1379 8

A CIP catalogue record of this title
is available from the British Library

Printed in Great Britain
by Scotprint Ltd , Musselburgh